W9-ANO-617

For Ingo and Bernhard

First published in the United States, Great Britain, Canada, Australia, and New Zealand
in 2011 by North-South Books Inc., an imprint of NordSüd Verlag AG, CH-8005 Zürich, Switzerland.
Distributed in the United States by North-South Books Inc., New York 10001.

Library of Congress Cataloging-in-Publication Data is available.
Printed in China by Leo Paper Products Ltd., Heshan, Guangdong, November 2010.
ISBN: 978-0-7358-4003-4 (trade edition)
1 3 5 7 9 • 10 8 6 4 2

www.northsouth.com

Iris Wewer

MY WILD SISTER AND ME

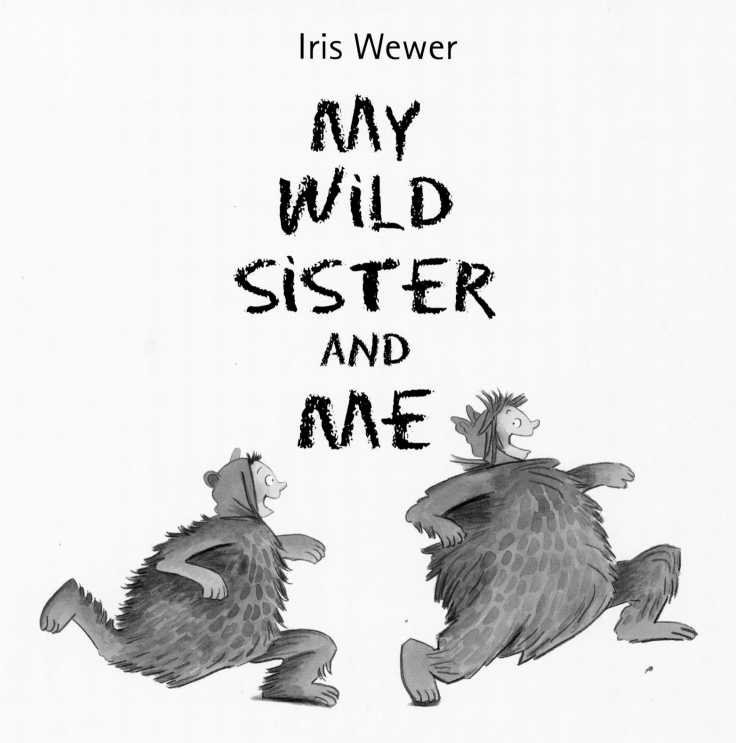

NorthSouth
New York / London

Sometimes my sister is a giraffe. She struts around and ignores me. When I tell her something, she doesn't listen to me. When I jump up and down in front of her, she doesn't look at me. When I shout as loud as I can **"DO YOU WANT TO PLAY?"** she doesn't answer me.

When my sister is a giraffe,
then I'm a smelly skunk.

Sometimes my sister is a big, cuddly bear. Then I'm a bear too, and we romp and stomp until the whole house shakes.

Sometimes my sister and I are birds with big, strong wings. When there's a storm outside, we soar high above the clouds.

One time my sister told me,
"The happiest animals in
the world are the rabbits.
When they hop around,
their hearts leap too
because they're so happy!"

So that day my sister and I
were rabbits. We bounced
through the field and the
woods until our hearts leaped
with happiness too.

We played Catch-the-Bunny . . .

. . . and had a real adventure. A fox wanted to eat us! He snarled at us and stared at us with his hungry eyes, but just at that moment . . .

. . . Penny from next door stuck her head into the room. "I'm going swimming," she told my sister. "Want to come with me?"

And they went, just like that. Right in the middle of our bunny adventure!
My sister didn't even say good-bye.

I sat on the porch for the whole afternoon. I didn't want to do anything.
I was a lonely bunny and not even a little bit happy.

The sun was already going down when my sister came home.

"Hi," she said, but I pretended not to hear her. I just ignored her.

I was really angry!
And I had a plan!

Right after dinner I crept into the bathroom
and took my sister's toothbrush.

I made sure nobody saw me.

Pretty soon a dangerous leopard was standing in front of me.

"WHERE IS MY TOOTHBRUSH?" she roared.

"I don't know," I said, and stared straight into her eyes.

My bunny ears were getting really hot and itchy, but I didn't scratch them.

Luckily I was wearing my
rabbit shoes—the ones that
make me run really fast and
don't leave any tracks.

"Look what I've got!"
I shouted, and the bunny
chase started, straight
out the front door . . .

. . . and across
the meadow . . .

. . . until my sister caught me. Her toothbrush flew out of
my hand and up through the air, higher and higher . . .

. . . until it landed in a bird's nest.
Getting it back was going to be tricky.

Then my sister said, "Can you hear that?" And I could.
Everything was silent! Giraffes and bears and birds and bunnies.
Moms and dads and boys and girls. Everybody was asleep.

So we crept back home.

When we were brushing our teeth, I asked my wild sister,
"Do you want to play Catch-the-Bunny again tomorrow?"

"Maybe," she said.